Ronnie Reid Can
Finally Read

Lisa Goodson

ISBN 978-1-64559-771-1 (Paperback)
ISBN 978-1-64559-772-8 (Hardcover)
ISBN 978-1-64559-773-5 (Digital)

Covenant Books, Inc.
11661 Hwy 707
Murrells Inlet, SC 29576
www.covenantbooks.com

For Jermaine, Alana, Taylor and all
the readers around the world!

1

Ronnie Reid was the only kid in his class who could not read at the age of three. His mother and father tried everything to help Ronnie to learn to read—flash cards in the morning and night, letter tiles and words on cards that he had to know by sight.

Mom would ask, "Ronnie, what sound does this letter make?"

Ronnie confused the *D*s with *B*s and would always hesitate. He forgot to lift his tongue when saying the *L* sound and wondered what the difference was between the *M* and *N* sound.

Mom sighed, "Will Ronnie ever learn to read?"
Dad replied, "He will, just wait and see."

As each year passed at school, students laughed and chanted, "Ronnie Reid can't read... Ronnie Reid can't read!"

7

They would say, "Ronnie, what's that word that we see? Oh, we forgot you're seven years old and still can't even read!"

Tears would swell up in his eyes…but he would look up at the ceiling so the tears wouldn't fall from his eyes. Ronnie wanted so badly to learn to read and comprehend. He began memorizing the stories so that he could pretend.

During reading time at school he'd sit in his comfy spot and keep his eyes in the book, although reading the words he could not but the pictures on the page he would look.

READING CENTER

With so many kids in his class he was able to fool them all at last. The credit for his cleverness was not his alone. He had to share it with his best friend Simone.

When the teacher asked, "What is the answer that shows what this story is mostly about?"

Simone would whisper, "Say *A*," to which Ronnie would repeat.

"Excellent!" his teacher would smile, showing her teeth.

Ronnie and Simone were a great pair. Homework they did together, and answers they always shared…until the worst day of their lives when they received the news.

Ronnie in class 301 and Simone in class 302 written clear as day on their final report card in June.

"What are we going to do?" they both asked.

Ronnie and Simone began to feel extremely blue. For Ronnie Reid still could not read, and Simone knew that number calculations she just couldn't do.

So they did what any smart kids would do. They agreed, "If you teach me, then I'll teach you."

That summer they ran and played as they did on any summer day. As they threw the ball Ronnie would count and ask, "How many did we throw in all?" While playing he would shout, "Count to sixty minus ten," and Simone began to calculate to find out where her counting would end.

Ronnie would say, "How many more rocks did I throw than you?"

Slowly Simone started to know what to do.

Simone would say, "Ronnie, I got this book from home about football." And they would read together, and Ronnie learned all about his favorite sport and facts that he had no idea of at all.

Other days Simone would bring magazines and comics to read. They'd both laugh so hard and slowly Ronnie began to read.

301

302

What interesting books have you read this summer?
Please discuss with a partner.

The beginning of the school year came so fast! Ronnie and Simone walked together until they split to go into their new class.

In class 301 the teacher asked the students to discuss any interesting books they had read. Ronnie discussed the characters in his books that he and Simone had read together. They were still fresh in his head.

Ronnie discussed the different genres of stories that he and Simone had read and how he loved humorous stories and stories about sports rather than only traditional stories instead.

Simone sat in 302 clinching the palm of her hand, and she could hear the pounding of her heart when Ms. Williams put the problem of the day for students to solve on the chart.

"How much farther did student A run than student B?"

Simone began to problem solve and realized that this problem was similar to one that she heard from Ronnie.

She was the first to raise her hand and share her solution, which was right!

Her teacher exclaimed, "Wow, great math thinking, that was out of sight!"

Even Mia, the mathematician in the school, said, "That was pretty cool!"

Ronnie and Simone walked home sharing stories about their day. They both had smiles from ear to ear on their faces. Pretending, Ronnie Reid no longer had to do. His knowledge of words and language grew and grew at a really fast speed. For Ronnie Reid finally knew how to read!

About the Author

Lisa Howerton Goodson spent many years in the education system as a New York City educator and a principal. She is passionate about reading and learning. She loves to spend time with her three children, traveling and singing karaoke. She also spends time with her dog Chloe, who by the way, she is still trying to potty train. Not an easy quest! Lisa spends much of her time brainstorming characters and creating stories for children to read. Sometimes even at work, she catches herself brainstorming fascinating characters and stories! Lisa's mission is to expand the boundaries of children's imagination. Sharing her gift of writing is her purpose and true calling. She lives in Long Island, New York, where most days you can find her curled up reading a good book or somewhere (couch, deck, airport, mall) doing what she loves best—writing!